Always be kind to others and remember to
Pay It Forward!

Gretchen Detora

Dave and Danny Pay It Forward is dedicated in memory of David L. Vaughan who lost his life in a car accident commuting to work on September 27, 2013. Dave, the main character in the story, is based on David Vaughan and how he lived his life: always helping his family, friends, and countless people who simply crossed his path. He was the epitome of all that is kind and good. David's positive energy and spirit was truly a light in the world. He was a devoted husband to his wife Kristen, and a loving father to his three young children Colin, Kevin, and Caroline.

- Gretchen Detora

www.mascotbooks.com

Dave and Danny Pay It Forward

For more information, please contact:
Mascot Books
560 Herndon Parkway #120
Herndon, VA 20170
info@mascotbooks.com

PRT0317B
Second Printing
ISBN-10: 1620866072
ISBN-13: 9781620866078

Printed in the United States

DAVE AND DANNY PAY IT FORWARD

GRETCHEN DETORA

ILLUSTRATED BY

JASON BOUCHER

Everyone in the neighborhood knew Dave Taylor by his friendly manner and the huge smile on his face. The kids called him Mr. T.

Whiffle ball games would turn into neighborhood parties the moment Dave joined in. All the kids cheered when Mr. T. stepped up to the plate. He could hit the ball straight through the trees.

When it was trash day in the neighborhood, Dave would be waiting there outside his house to help Gus, the trash man, dump his trash barrels into the back of his truck.

"You sure make my day, Dave," smiled Gus. "You are the only one who helps me each week. If everyone was like you, our world would be a better place."

Dave just smiled and said, "Thank you, Gus." He truly made Gus feel like he was the most important person in the world.

Gus shook his head slightly and smiled as he climbed into his truck and headed for the next house on his route.

One day, Dave's son, Danny, asked his dad why he helped Gus dump their trash into the trash truck.

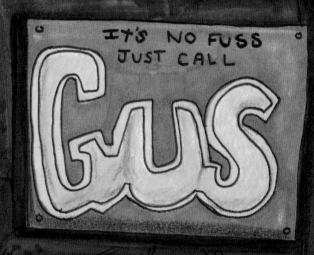

IT'S NO FUSS
JUST CALL

Gus

1·555·TRASH

"Danny, it's just what you do. You help people out," explained Dave. "Let's go for a ride. We are going on an adventure and I have a surprise in store too." There was a twinkle in his eye and Danny loved surprises. He knew it would be fun because his dad was the most fun dad in the whole wide world.

"Dad, you had better tell Mom where we're going. She always says you're a free spirit. I guess that means you do what you like to do," chuckled Danny.

Dave had a big grin on his face. "Your mom knows me a bit too well," laughed Dave.

Dave and Danny jumped into the truck and off they went. Dave had a plan but he never really knew what would happen until he was on his way. It made the adventure all the more exciting. This was going to be a day that Danny would remember for a long time.

"Okay, Danny, our first stop is the pet store," said Dad.

"Are we getting a dog?" questioned Danny.

"Well, not exactly."

As they got out of the car, a woman was coming out of the pet store, struggling with a large bag of dog food.

"Let me get that for you," Dave said with a smile. He carried it over to her car and loaded it in her trunk.

A smile lit up her face. "If only more people were like you, our world would be a better place. Thank you so much, young man."

Dave laughed and said, "Well, calling me young man just made my day. You are most welcome. Have a wonderful day."

The woman shook her head slightly and smiled as she watched Dave and Danny walk into the pet store.

In the pet store, Dave and Danny walked around, looking at all the animals. There were colorful fish, squawking birds, furry bunnies, meowing kittens, and dogs wagging their tails. They weren't there to buy a pet, though. Dave grabbed a cart and loaded it with bags of dog and cat food.

"But Dad, we don't have any animals."

Dave smiled and wheeled the cart to the counter. He paid for the food and brought the bags to the truck. Danny climbed in the passenger seat and off they went. In a short while, Dave turned into a driveway. Danny didn't know where they were.

"We're here, Danny. I need some help getting these bags out of the truck. We're at the animal shelter to donate these bags of food," explained Dave.

Dave and Danny brought the bags of food in and the woman sitting at the desk smiled at them. "Thank you so much for your thoughtful donation. We always need food for our animals and we depend on people like you to help us out. You both have made our world a better place today. What a great example you are to your son."

They both smiled and said thank you.

"It's our pleasure," said Dave.

When Dave and Danny were back in the truck, Danny turned to his dad. "Dad, you really do help a lot of people. I can tell the people you help are always happy."

"Danny, it's about our inner spirit. It's the connection that people have with each other. When I help another person, it really makes me feel good inside too. Speaking of that, didn't I say that I have a surprise for you?"

"Yes, you did, Dad," Danny said with excitement.

"This Sunday afternoon, the Eagles are playing the Wildcats in hockey and you and I are going to the game!"

"No way, Dad! Are you serious?"

"As serious as I could ever be," laughed Dave.

"Hey Dad, did you hear the Eagles have a new mascot? It's a real live eagle. How cool is that?"

"Yeah, that's pretty cool. Speaking of hockey, we have to get you signed up to play this year."

They passed Danny's school on the way. "Hey, Danny, there's good old South School. What an awesome school you go to."

In a short time, they pulled into the local hockey shop.

Dave's buddy, Brad, was the manager of the store. Brad and Dave went to high school together, playing hockey all four years. They were a force to be reckoned with on the ice in their day.

"Hey, Dave. Hey, Danny. What's up, you guys?" Brad called out from behind the counter. "Can you believe it's sign-up time again? You coaching Danny this year?"

"Absolutely, wouldn't dream of not coaching. You know I think I was born with skates on," laughed Dave.

"Yeah me too," said Brad.

Just then, Dave noticed out of the corner of his eye a young boy about Danny's age looking at skates. He thought he might go to Danny's school but he didn't look familiar.

"Pretty nice skates you're looking at there, champ," said Dave.

The young boy dropped his head down and looked away. Dave knew in his gut that something was wrong.

"Hey buddy, are you okay?" asked Dave.

"I just want to play hockey, that's all," he said sadly.

Dave wanted to boost his spirits. "Do you have a favorite team?" he asked.

The young boy looked up, smiled, and said, "I love the Eagles. My cousin's friend plays on their team."

"No way! That's our favorite team too."

"Aren't you the new kid at school? Your name is Ryan, right?" asked Danny. He recognized him from the class across the hall.

"Yes, I'm Ryan. We just moved here but I can't play hockey because my dad is sick and can't work right now. My mom said we don't have the money," said Ryan.

"Where's your mom?" questioned Danny.

"She's next door at the drugstore picking up medicine for my dad. She'll be here in a minute."

Just then, Ryan saw his mom walk through the door. Seeing her son with Dave and Danny, she had a look of concern on her face. "Is everything okay?" she asked.

"Yes, it's just fine. Hi, my name is Dave and this is my son, Danny. We live here in town and we just had the pleasure of meeting your son. Ryan tells me he's a big hockey fan."

"That he is! Hi, my name is Charlotte. It's a pleasure to meet you, Dave and Danny. We just moved here."

"Ryan was telling me that. Charlotte, can I ask you something?"

"Certainly, what is it?"

"I would like to know if Ryan could join our hockey team. I'm the coach and we have a couple of open spots on the team," informed Dave.

Charlotte looked down for a moment. "I am not sure we can afford it at this time, Dave. I know Ryan is disappointed but I am doing the best I can under the circumstances," Charlotte replied sadly.

Dave spoke up. "Ryan was looking at skates. A friend of mine just gave me a brand new pair that I know will fit him. Don't worry about the sign-up fee or anything else. It's all taken care of. I can pick him up for practice too."

Charlotte couldn't believe what she was hearing. Ryan was beaming from ear to ear.

"Dave, really this is too much. I don't even know you and you are doing all this for us?"

"Charlotte, let me say something. What is this world all about if we can't help each other. I see the biggest smile on Ryan's face, and you know what? His smile has made my day."

"But how can we repay you for this?" asked Charlotte.

"I'll tell you what," said Dave, "it's called giving back and when you find that you are in a position to give back to someone, then you can do it too. Pay it forward, as they say."

"Dave, thank you so much for your warmth and generosity. There aren't enough people like you around but you certainly have taught me a big lesson today. And Ryan, too."

"Happy to do it for you, really, I am. Ryan, we will pick you up for our first practice at 9 a.m. Saturday morning. Deal?"

"Deal," smiled Ryan.

"Wait a minute, Dad," said Danny. "Hey Ryan, we have two tickets to the Eagles and Wildcats game on Sunday. We want you to have them."

Dave turned to his son with a look of wonder. Danny gave him a wink.

"Yes we do, Ryan. I actually have the tickets with me. Here you go," he said as he handed him two tickets.

"Like father, like son." Charlotte had tears in her eyes.

When they got in the truck to drive home, Dave turned to Danny and said, "You made me the proudest father today. What you did was very generous."

"I think you are teaching me, Dad. It's just what you do—you help people out."

At that moment they were driving past Stachey's Pizza, Danny's favorite pizza shop. "Hey, I'm starving. Can we get pizza for lunch?"

"Absolutely, Danny. Whatever you want."

"Double cheese with pepperoni?"

"You got it!" Dave said with a big smile.

In loving memory of David L. Vaughan

www.vaughanfamilytrust.com

ABOUT THE AUTHOR

Gretchen Detora works as an Instructional Assistant in a second grade classroom at South Elementary School in Andover, Massachusetts. As an author, Gretchen writes her children's stories with the intention of inspiring others to find positive solutions in everyday life. This has always been Gretchen's focus in her own life as well. While raising her son, Ryan, she taught him the importance of giving back to others and how just one person can make a significant difference in the world. Gretchen also brings this important message to her students at South Elementary School. It is her hope that the positive messages in her stories will reach many more. Gretchen lives in North Andover, Massachusetts, with her husband, Arthur.

ABOUT THE ILLUSTRATOR

Jason Boucher is an artist and mason. He has been in construction for sixteen years but he's been an artist most of his life. He never took a lesson and is pretty much self-taught. He's married to his beautiful wife, Erika, and they have a beautiful daughter, Kayla, and two handsome sons, Beau and Blake. His goal is to be a full-time illustrator and finally throw his work boots away.